IMPOSSIBL

Also by Michael Glover

Measured Lives

IMPOSSIBLE HORIZONS

Michael Glover

SINCLAIR-STEVENSON

First published in Great Britain in 1995
by Sinclair-Stevenson
an imprint of Reed International Books Ltd
Michelin House, 81 Fulham Road, London SW3 6RB
and Auckland, Melbourne, Singapore and Toronto

A CIP catalogue record for this book
is available at the British Library

ISBN 1 85619 612 7

Typeset by Deltatype Ltd, Ellesmere Port, Cheshire
Printed and bound in Great Britain by
Cox & Wyman Ltd, Reading

To Dorothy and Honor

Grateful acknowledgement is made to the
publications in which some of these poems first
appeared: *Acumen*, *Agenda*, the *Independent*, *Outposts*;
and, especially, to Dagger Press for poems that were
published in *Measured Lives* (1994).

As pearls from grit,
So poems from words
Debased and sullied,
Frail, absurd.

Contents

I

The ancient measure of the llama's thigh

The Ancient Travails of the Word-Smith

So many old words living obscure lives
Without even a wish to shame the streets
Into acknowledging their enterprise,
Their youthfulness – despite longevity.

They're busy at the things they love to do –
Creating wordscapes, tall against their sky,
So sleek and thin and infinitely true,
As ancient-modern as the llama's thigh.

I glimpsed them through the glass one afternoon.
I tried the words against my tongue and sighed.
No wonder that they build them in that room.
No wonder that it's closed against the light.

Sister Wrenshaw's Hymnal

Can I ever hope to catch up with the present?
There is so much of it, and it never stops coming.
Already yesterday's unread newspaper has dwindled
To a blizzard of soot flecks in the windy grate.
At the window, turning, I catch sight of tomorrow's faces,
Looking so fresh and so ready to fight off the future
Because, they mouth through the glass, it is evil,
Being the opposite of the good which is us, here, today . . .
Is then tomorrow, in their somewhere, today?
I return to the fire in hopeless metaphysical disarray.
And then a door wrenches open at my back,
A door which seems to resemble the door
That hung in that very same doorway in someone's yesterday –
A pitted, old, badly fitting door,
All thumb prints beside the sneck, grease stains,
And rusted nail heads of a most awkward shape.
Through that door passes a multitude of beings and things –
The flat iron from the attic, Sister Wrenshaw's Hymnal,
And the washboard from grandmother's sink.
No one is carrying anything.
It all proceeds at head height, bobbing through the air.
And behind all this welter of things come the people,
Bringing up the rear.
Who are they all? Do I know them?
And is it firm ground that I stand on here?

The Rat of Poetry

Poetry is what creeps in unregarded after the
clamour has died away. It is the rat who ventures
into the dining room after nightfall; after the
party is over; after the last drunken guests
have taken their separate ways home, pleased
with themselves for everything that they have
said and everything that they have refrained
from saying. It is then that the rat comes,
with due caution at first; but, within seconds,
increasing confidence, skidding across platters,
nudging pink crumbs of icing with its nose towards
the abyss beyond the table's edge; lashing the linen
table cloth with the hefty whip of its tail. We must
learn to look this creature in the face without
fear; to accept the image of ourselves which we see
reflected in the glint of its black, bulbous eye; to
live with the discomfiting knowledge that it is he –
and no other – who is gnawing at our innards.

Description of a House

The long, slow defiance of cold bedrooms.
The perfect plausibility of stairs.
The pent embarrassment of shuttered closets.
The waiting and the waiting of the chair.

The unexpected heartache of small windows.
The pleasurable fever of the leaf.
The nasty little promise of a knife edge.
The consequence of air, whirled into grief.

The nature, lackadaisical, of scissors.
One hot, remembered corner – all my life . . .
The coming and the going and the coming.
The filling and the emptying. The blight.

The tearing down of walls. The stroke of hammers.
The fissuring of glass. The shapes of mouths.
A sledge's dirty burial, with ashes.
The gradual retreat. The candle out.

Back Yard Scene, Sheffield 1958

My mother ran and whisked the washing in.
The soot flakes fell, black snow from a grey sky.
The beer barrels came trundling along,
With surly men in aprons by their side.

The shelter that had kept the Germans out
Stood staunch and ugly by the lavvy doors.
We crept in there to hear our voices shout
Out swear words, tell real ghost stories, lose balls.

An outside lavvy's not a bad thing though,
Especially when the greens make you feel sick.
I stuffed them in my cheeks like hamsters do,
And shot them out in bits. The water flicked.

The Warm Wash of Optimism

You are old now and three parts infirm.
You stare at a child. Its jumping gives you hope.
No, the child itself *is* hope, injecting into time
A marvellous warm wash of optimism
So that you read things quite differently,
And learn again the habit of
Smiling into the light.

You are old now and a whole one quarter hale.
With the help of a stick you speed down the gennel
Behind the child, who jingles his bell and wails.
Some sense of a new day is on the rise.
You stop by the roadside, both of you,
To let the funeral procession pass by.
Let them die, you think,
Restraining the child by the collar
As if you are reining in a colt,
Let them all go and die.
Then you bolt.

The Clown's Particular Benediction

They have set about to manufacture
Some old, well-tried coastal town
With one toe in the sea-mist,
A shingle beach, and a single impassive clown.
First, they remove the ancient guildhall
From the central square of a sequestered village
Somewhere high up in the downs,
Parting, with the utmost delicacy, lath from rib
Until there is nothing left
But a glorious, old-world picture of the thing
Lodged amidst the mind's eye's wanderings,
In all the splendour of its ancient days –
And, of course, the smoking heap of it.
Second, an old stone jetty will almost certainly be required
For the swift town dogs to race along
With their owners coming after, shouting:
Danger! Danger! Don't be so wild!
Of people, they will need four –
The mayor (old, sun-struck and a touch bemused),
An estate agent (mildly alcoholic in his grizzled beard),
Miss Sarah, who will dubbin her step with righteous fervour,
And, last but not least, me.
I shall offer my own particular benediction
Before they set it down.
I am the clown.

The House Above the Ashokan Reservoir

The mellowness of wood on those broad stairs
That made a gentle twist up to the light
Of living space so full of air it seemed
Not comfortable, no, but merely right . . .

Within that space the sun made gentle play,
But not until the evening, when the light
That danced upon the reservoir's broad face
Shone up into our eyes. And then we bathed.

But was it not the colour of that wood,
The wood he'd used for stairs and parquet floor,
That gave the house its special atmosphere,
An atmosphere of ochre to the core?

And what did ochre in that wood suggest –
If that is not too definite a word?
A balm that soothes anxieties away;
A something that approximates to rest.

Dunfermline

They buried the many amongst the few
A few wet weeks and some heartache ago.
I counted up seven of them travelling through,
A pair from Dunfermline, the others unknown.

They told me: it's luck, that's what's goading us on,
Those seven fine men, though so shifty of eye.
They told me: one glimpse of the sea and we're done,
That few with so many, the many a lie.

When they came to the field that was known for the spot –
Was it that many weeks ago, that many sons? –
They threw down their picks and broke open their crocks.
By six they were snoring, and down crept the sun.

It was then that the many, the silent ones, struck –
The dead can't abide to be left on their own.
It was then that a bunch of them sprung – o, the luck
Had turned tail again. Night's work was done.

And now, in wan sunlight, the many, the few
Embrace in the earth again, peaceful at last.
But what of the boy that ran, he without shoes?
'Dunfermline,' he said, that one word, to the grass.

A Fine Coating of Green Slime

Speak cleanly as if your mouth has just been rinsed in
fresh spring water.
If there is lime in it still, try the colander, the sieve or
something finer.
You need just a little lime for your own health's sake – but not
too much, of course.
Now taste your tongue. Does it taste good – or is there a fine
coating of green slime
That prevents you telling the truth about your day?
Take a knife edge and scrape it off into the sink.
Now you can join in the play.
You are to play the part of a dirty, polluted stream
In which animals and fish float upside down with open eyes,
Neither quite dead nor properly alive.
Drink some water from the tap to get a taste for the part.
Now paint your tongue with green from the paint box
Which was one of Santa's gifts to the children,
That Santa we used to see with worn-out shoes
Who wandered round and round and round the park.

The Sealed Jar

That man who has the eyes to see at night,
Combing the distance for the merest light,
Will understand that seeking does not end
When people disappear around a bend.

And yet to follow is to risk abuse.
Far better to show caution – or the truth
May prove too horrible to contemplate.
Far better to arrive a little late.

And yet to go is to predict an end,
An end that may throw caution to the winds.
So, best of all, seal eyes inside this jar.
All roads that go away must go too far.

The Kingdom of Old Horses

This kingdom of old horses –
Broken-backed nags, lean, sad fillies –
Is being dismembered,
Carcase by cracked, bloated carcase,
And I shall run back to my village.

Not in order to tell them.
Not in order to account for their ways –
Merely to be there, kicking, alive again,
Free of it all . . . to count my days.

Here they are now, on my hand here,
One two three four five six and seven . . .
I count them on these fingers still remaining –
One for every fine horse in my heaven.

The Message Bearers

They go, alone, to plead for what I am.
Sometimes I see, at other times, I'm seen.
Their silence is a warning to my life
Not to disturb the anchor of the dream.

They weave in air, beneath a hectic sky.
Two hands reach out, as if intent to grasp.
The paper waits, now somnolent, now still.
What comes will come unbidden – life, its task.

There is a noise of waiting – pent, the throb
That rocks the dozy carriage on the line.
Outside, the summer landscape peels away –
Those faded, heat-struck fields, topped by tall sky.

Someday, I know, I'll bring all this inside,
Arranging it like teacups on a tray.
The clatter of that busy, futile work
Will make it seem a job fit for the day.

Questionable Answers

Q. There will always be the one left behind, at home,
Who did not quite achieve what you achieved.
But what *did* you see?
A. I saw as far as the next hill and beyond.
I stood on the very summit of that hill and breathed . . .
Q. And what did you *see* from that awe-inspiring vantage point?
A. I saw another hill that seemed molten
In the dying light of the sun.
Q. And did that hill resemble something strange and new?
A. It resembled, most of all, a hill.
One hill resembles, most of all, another hill.
Q. And then what did you do? Did you rejoice?
A. I turned my back
And sought the track back home.
Q. And did you find it?
A. Well, am I not here?
Q. Some part of you is here. No doubt of that.
But it was dark. How did you see?
A. The sweets that I had dropped along the way
Winked up at me like cat's eyes until day.

The Poem and its Audience

Somewhere there is a person waiting for the poem's arrival,
Hands jammed into pockets, staring out of a window at
nothing at all.
Some part of the day he spends usefully, taming an allotment.
Later he may riffle a newspaper or examine a wall.

It is on that wall, as it happens, that the poem has been written,
A sometime empty wall now alive with the life of signs.
It is on that wall that he reads it, a little stiff from the allotment,
Flexing his finger joints, opening and closing his eyes.

What does the poem do, the one that he is reading?
How does it make itself known to him in a singular way?
Written as it is for the man who spends half a lifetime
bent double in allotments,
Another quarter with newspapers, jammed deep into a chair,
And the final portion conjuring things from the tall, divisive
nothings that some call walls,
It is almost bound to persuade.

Portrait of an Absent Father

He had been so unnaturally gentle for so long,
Sweeping the floor with his hair,
Seeming not to care
About dishes heaped up or tumbled in the sink;
Appearing not to think
Whether the day had ended as it began,
With the cries of children filling up the least little space
In the ear and in the air.

He had been so strangely languid for so long,
With that shock of lank blond hair
Falling so far;
The soft, sweet voice creeping through fairy tales
In old books whose bindings,
A little tatty like his waistcoat and trousers,
Gave a sense of rooted belonging
In some magical somewhere
That was not here.

He had been so present in his absence for so long
That to find him standing there
Barking out orders,
Marshalling children in corners, through doorways,
Seemed like another was speaking;
Another whose being had been there, inside him, all along;
Waiting at the bottom of the stairs,
For the child to descend
And be told:
Go away now. Act your age.
I am your father. Care as I cared.

A Protected Child

the threat of what was never thought or said
the fear of its approaching some day soon
the consequences smeared across the walls
the knowledge that what matters is this room

and all that it contains of what I am
the little that I was, may come to be
so little that my eyes cannot adjust
to all the bigness that will threaten me

when father chooses, flinging wide the door,
letting the air in, all that that will mean,
the flies that will come skimming down its slopes,
the flies, the blood, the messages, the dreams

The Promise of the Widow's Mite

Edgar's gone down. I'm left alone
To face it all in these four walls
Of breeze block, patched with sand, clay, dung.
If this is life, I've seen it all –

The misery of want, the pain,
The deaths of children in the womb,
The loss of comrades, former friends
Who always left a mite too soon.

There'd be a question in the air,
A look that I would scarcely see,
Some gesture of a wrist, a call
To vengeance, purity – past grief.

A donkey brays. It's break of day.
I see them fighting on the cliffs –
Although they're far ahead of me,
Too far for me to notice if . . .

The Starkest Deprivations Fix the Truth

The objects wander, circling the field.
A cloud swims down, close-shadowing the grass.
Somewhere – and then: again! – faint clops of hoof . . .
The starkest deprivations fix the truth.

The man leans, sewing, skirts below the knee.
A woman beats her heart out on a drum.
One hawkish eye adjusts above the roof.
The starkest deprivations fix the truth.

An ear gapes open to the strangest tune.
The lamp makes ready, seriously blue.
And as regards the mysteries of proof:
The starkest deprivations fix the truth.

The Plenitude of Nothing

Now here is nothing. And it's all there is.
Observe its movements – if it moves at all.
A rock's the best of vantage points, I'd say.
The plainsman's vision is obscured by walls.

How do you take it now that you've arrived?
Are you at all . . . at all . . . discomfited?
Is it some piecemeal thing, the one you've lived,
Your life, I mean, that 'very special gift'?

I know you can't. And therefore I won't ask.
Let's look together – if we look at all.
The other way – some say the best there is –
Is to face backwards and pretend to call.

These Devilish Days

Where is that ungainly measure of the truth
That, oh so long ago, we used to use?
Its stock, in the palm, seemed a near perfect fit –
The warmth and the smoothness of old, tried wood –
Yes, that must have been it . . .
How *did* we use it though? What did we *do*?
Was it a single plain swing through the air –
Some movement like a flourish – straight across and through?
Or did it turn half back on itself in a stealthy, rising curve,
Less machine than bird?
My greatest fear, of course, is not so much that it is lost –
Few things are not in these devilish days –
But that, having fallen into the oily hands
Of those who deal and dice with contraband,
It may have vanished somewhere
Where nothing of that kind has ever been understood –
The many simple uses to which one may put old, hard wood.
Who knows? It may – as I write these very words –
Be rotting beneath the ground
Or, worse, someone who will forever be unknown to me
May be misusing it – upside down.

The Towering of Circumstances

The circumstances loved us all the same –
that broken wall, the way it fell about;
the match-box tower, the sheerness of its walls;
the confidence of children when they shout.

We passed on by, exulting in the wish
to swim in all these elements of gain.
We had no money in our pockets then –
but who needs money with such open claims

to lavish love and, later, snatch it back;
to grasp what is ungraspable by greed;
to build that tower, room upon tiny room,
and then lie down, spent by our burning need?

The Presence of Porlock

Is Porlock still alive in me?
Is it a place, a man, a tower,
A dream I had the other day
Of hammers striking on the hour?

If Porlock comes now, will he stay?
And should I stop and chat with him?
Will what he tell me lead me here?
Or is *this* here, and he mere whim?

Did Porlock ever touch my eyes?
Were those his fingers that I felt?
Was he the man he claimed to be?
Or is he really someone else?

If Porlock lives the way he said,
Does that affect this sweep of fields
That rises from the old stream bed
And slowly, ghost-like, disappears?

Hope of a Kind

With every new day, hope of a kind returns –
That chord struck by the sun at the window,
Or some smaller measure, at the rose-red lip of a vase.
Are there arrears in love to be recouped? It is not too late.
Concentrate on all the things that you have ever been –
Those attacks of giddy youthfulness or, now, in this chair,
Mending a seam. Will you take flight again?
Will you make your mark in some high room?
No, you are small, much smaller, than you once were,
And the little of you that there is
Is to be preserved – like the last pickle in the jar.
Hope of a kind *has* returned to you.
Clasp it to your own cold bosom. Do not go far.

At the Underground Station

I am the fourth horseman of the apocalypse,
Though mountless, slipshod and beyond reproof.
I am the fourth (or fifth) horseman of the apocalypse,
Brilliantly caparisoned beneath the wide sky's roof.
Have you not noticed my gait as I stride
Between here and there, visor atilt to match
  the sun's fierce gleam?
Have you paid no regard to the reticulations of my mail,
The fineness of it all, the strange music that it makes
When I run nail across best steel?
I have for hair, horse hair – and who would gainsay that?
I have for boots, *bottines* – and who would blench at that?
It is the task of the fourth horseman of the apocalypse
To stand guard at all four corners of this kingdom of winds.
For some, that would prove an insuperable burden;
But to me, blessed as I am with a pair of fine-honed blades,
  well-preened wings
And an o'erbrimming measure of bravura when I rise on the
  slumped shoulders of these underlings,
Everything is possible – and just a little more.
If you should wish me hung, drawn and quartered,
You need only open that great drooling mouth of yours
  and roar.
For know this: I am embezzled up to and beyond the elbows.
In fact, I am at war.

Incident on a Warm Evening in the Cotswolds

When I saw the bed humped unnaturally high,
I knew it to be an animal.
When I picked off the cover in the half-light
Of evening, and saw the limbs stir, resisting me,
I knew it had to die.
When I raised the honed instrument above my head,
And saw the crooked, extended arm on the wall,
And heard that first, tiny cry,
I knew there would be no appeasement of any kind
Because the beast that I had in mind
Deserved no appeasement and understood
Nothing at all.
When I stowed the pieces in their appointed places,
Having first cleansed my hands and wiped them dry,
Back and front, on my thighs,
I spoke, for the first time, out loud to the room,
Telling it all that it had seen and heard,
But re-making its visions
In such a way as to fashion permanence
From the forgetfulness of the passing moment:
There are those appointed, the words ran,
To end as they began;
There are those destined, the words continued,
To meet at both ends of their lives –
To meet death at the moment of living,
And life at the moment they die.
And then I, in my turn,
Having prepared for this too, died –
Though to the world and its judgements,
Better or otherwise,
I may seem to have remained alive.

The Special Relationship with the Poem

In order to fall in love with a poem,
You must first enter into the spirit of its special circumstances –
There is nothing worse than to be ill-dressed for an occasion:
Epauletted, when bangles – or a beard – are to the point;
Bewoggled, when the Milanese silk tie is the only proper form.
Every poem is like a love story – on its day.
On other days, approach it sidelong, wistfully,
As if all time might slip away unnoticed
In some Florentine *pensione*, lambrettas stretch-farting in the
street below.
By now, you have come to the tall, forbiddingly baroque gate of
the preface.
Yes, words have eased into a fitful flow.
In order to fall in love with a poem,
You must take the measure of its – and your – style.
Are you circumlocutorily Jamesian today?
Do you measure inches by the mile?
Do not be dismayed by the sight of a high cairn of words.
No poem reaches further than the dimensions of your dictionary.
Shake that dictionary out onto your lap,
And re-assemble them all until you have it –
Apt, expectant, fully-formed,
The perfect mirror-likeness of that very poem
Which had thought to have you in its thrall.
You yourself are as tall as your neighbour's poem.
You are its covert subject-matter.
In little, you are its all.

The Maddening Half-Glimpse of Pinpricks

Life seemed always too short and too difficult
To accommodate anything that might wish to be said
Of lasting consequence.
He therefore concluded, quite early on,
That the better road was silence.
The air proved higher and cleaner,
With an uninterrupted view of the clouds
And a sense of space everywhere.
Not once was he aroused
By pinpricks glimpsed on the horizon line,
Zig-zagging unpredictably here and there.
He took them for so many motes in his eye.

The Release

Wide-eyed, he came and knelt beside the tree.
The tree gave shelter, though he shivered still.
Just then he thought: why must it still be *me*
Who suffers for this general ill?

He felt himself preposterous out there –
Those clothes he wore, too large, too thin, too fine.
Who was it that had dropped them by the chair?
What motive did she have for being kind?

In memory, he saw a little girl,
A sister, his, her arms around a tree.
But was it this one? That he did not know.
Nor why they'd let him go and called him free.

Just Being at West Hurley

When I stand apart from myself
And think of the day as it is
Deciding to be – that note of
Jocularity in the air,
A general wanting breathing
Through the trees, I think of your form –
Tensile, seemly, rare,
The very picture of all love's
Approximate forgiveness for
The two of us, together now,
Just being there.

The Decision

This morning, in the flat, murderous light of summer,
To be what one had never seemed to be
Could be an answer.
And so he quit, leaving the door ajar,
And pushed the pram, at speed, into the local park.

Snow Lines

To climb the steps
Is not to know
A door that opens
Onto snow.

To speak a word
Is not some quest
For miracles
Of wantonness.

And yet it is.
These things are so.
See how they couple
In the cold.

The Known Circumstances

A tall, pale man seen running by a hedge.
A heap of clothes – or had it been a stone?
Two words exchanged in haste. Dark laughter. Sun.
A snow flurry – so quickly past and gone.

The early darkness of a winter's night.
A square of light, gloom-yellow through the trees.
And in that light – a pendant silhouette
Slow-shifting sideways on some indoors breeze.

The Urn at Twilight

Today there was some loss of natural light,
Which had its own small impact on delight.

He lurched about the room, a stumbling bear,
Displacing cups, the sewing-bench, a chair.

But when he reached the window, he sat down
And feigned alertness to all things around:

The world that breathed beyond his window ledge –
A flat burnish of fields, the waiting hedge

That always huddled in the corner there
As if preparing for his stony stare.

On this new day his eyes seemed to reach out
And the whole world fall open with a shout.

At least, that's how it seemed, when he returned
To thinking of these things, and clutched the urn.

The Spectator

The moment raced away and he was left
With memories of a bench, the sea, a dog;
Which made him think: who's guilty of the theft
Of faces, *his* face, looming through the fog?

And so he tried again, and conjured words,
Words he had spoken, gestures, winning smiles.
But still they seemed like disembodied things –
The Cheshire Cat was up to its strange wiles . . .

And so he spoke his name into the air.
The hill that he was facing lobbed it back.
The hill behind him drove it back again.
And he was left spectating at a match.

Miami Cool Kids TV Rap

Hi! I'm Mami, and this is Cuba.
Hi! I'm Danny, and this is Miami.
Half the people in Miami, they speak Spanish.
Half the kids in Miami have braces on their teeth –
Get a glint of those braces: cool . . .
Get a glint of those braces – cool
As the roller blades on South Beach.
That's the way to get about, get about, get about –
By the cool blue waters of Miami beach!

Miami is all beach and blue blue water.
And so is Cuba, where they all speak Spanish.
I'm going to show you Miami in two and one half minutes –
Fast enough and cool enough for your TV!
You can only do that on roller blades.
You can only do that if you're a real cool dude – like me!
Now listen to the throb of the beat.
Now listen to the throb of the beat

As I show you Cuba,
Embedded down deep, here in Miami,
Here in the cool blue waters of Miami
Where I can see them all, all my family,
Out there, swimming, waving from the sea,
Washed up, wrecked up, spewing out water,
Washed up, wrecked up, floating free
In the cool blue waters of cool Miami,
In the cool blue waters of the living sea . . .

Are they really coming to America?
And will I know them when they come?
And will this make a difference to me?
Oh yes. Oh no. Oh yes. Oh no. Ho hum. Ho hum.
What really makes a difference are the waters of Miami.
What really makes a difference are the braces on my teeth –

All that dentistry! . . . Washed up, wrecked up, spewing out
water,
Washed up, wrecked up, bits floating free . . .

Papa is a man with a long grey beard.
Stays home, angry, watches TV.
Some time he shouts. Most time he's dumb.
But when he shouts, he says this: come, come, come.
Come you people, come away.
Come you people, come away.
Come Tinto, come Sanchez, come to me,
Don't get lost in the dirty sea,
Don't get drowned in the dying sea.

But he don't see the waters of Miami.
He stays home and combs his beard.
No, he don't see what I can see –
The waters of Miami, so cool and blue and free . . .
Now listen to the throb of being me,
Listen to the throb of being me –
All me!

Beyond Recognition

The poetry arrived a bit too soon.
I wasn't ready – nor were all the rest,
The one with open mouth, all shaving cream;
That blowsy one, too sleepy to be dressed.
The postman heaved them in a tight black sack.
Nothing had spilled. Containment was the word.
We claimed them, bit by bit, a tricky test
For the most indefatigable bird.
I scarcely understood the words I'd used.
I didn't recognise their style, that lisp.
And then I chanced upon one phrase that flew:
'Tuxedos wrestle with an armoured fist . . .'

The Ritual Humiliation of the City of London

London, step down into this grave. Lie flat.
Now close your eyes as if you meant to die.
You have two ears? Here's paper. Block them up.
That mouth hole too – quickly! Noses don't sigh.

London, where did you get that livid bruise?
Costumiers' invention knows no bounds.
Such pale, sad, trembling hands . . . Bind on these gloves.
Just do it – round and round and round and round.

Now stay quite still. *Don't* listen with those ears.
I'll cut your tongue off if you thrust it out.
It's just a small, thin, black thing anyway . . .
It's *not*? It's *pink* and *fat*? Try then. You shout . . .

The Disappearance of the Child

If Christ then is our only God,
Where does this leave that other boy,
The one our Mary loved so much,
She snatched him – like a playmate's toy –

And ran in frenzy through the streets,
The bundle tucked beneath her shawl,
And never said one word to God
Lest he should start to rage and bawl . . .

And now he's lost. She can't begin
To think what happened to the child
Who was her favourite tiny boy
With angel's hair and angel's wiles . . .

The outdoors room

Each life has its own separate balcony
To which a man or a woman ascends
From the fury of the office or the bedroom
To sip at the sweetness of air thinning down
From everywhere and nowhere,
Yet never too soon.

On that separate balcony,
A man or a woman comes to know what it is
Not to speak,
Nor to gesticulate or fume,
Merely to partake of
Some sense of light and space,
Fashioning from piecemeal rumination
The perfect outdoors room.

Looking down from that separate balcony,
He or she may see hastening
Many ill-defined persons or things.
Some appear to be seeking heavy brass rings
To which a foot, arm or finger might be tethered;
Others are more attentive to
The grace notes of evening winging.

The Singing Clown

I am the singing clown and I am about to die.
A beach such as this one, with its pebbles worked smooth
by the sea, is as good a place to die as any other.
I can scoop out a resting place for my head if father will not allow
me to lie across his knees, which I would much prefer.
I am a singing dying clown, and this morning the sea is singing
back to me – but not in so many words.
Its voice is ugly because its mouth is perpetually gargling
salt-sea water.
My body will be pickled in brine like the tinned sardines
That we buy here so cheaply from the supermarket.
My coffin will be sardine-tin-shaped and made from
shiny, sun-reflecting metal.
It will gently rust away on the sea's bottom, shunned by the
fish-hook-headed garfish, the squid with his gigantic,
looming eye, the frenzied schools of whitebait
That prefer the security of the harbour to the wider mouths of
the open sea.
I am the singing dying clown, but my salt-stiff golden hair will be
preserved unto eternity.
From its strands will be fashioned a rope ladder that will reach
Up to the crazed blue of a morning unvexed by cloud.
It is the late autumn of my tender young life, and the sun
lours down
Irrespective of what or whom I am becoming.
All day, in spirit, I am already asleep underground, absorbing
the greater goodnesses
Of moles and poets.

The I is instrumental

Odourless, pure, incorrigible facts
Assail me, of a morning, when I act
To clear the rubbish from the pipes downstairs.
They come between the action and the prayer.

What *do* I pray? That I might simply be
The fully human vessel I call me,
Nothing extraneous, nothing too untoward –
A single shaft of light that pours and pours . . .

And then the facts breeze in, so tidy, small and good,
Asking me why I thought I'd understood
The nature of the person with the name
That corresponds to mine. Was I insane?

Is that a question to be asked of me?
Had they seen in the minstrels' gallery
That constitutes the space behind my eyes –
Those broken-necked guitars, the stricken drum, and,
amidst those pale, cold limbs, that *fife*?

Patience, infinitely divisible

Days crowd out days.
The men have gathered.
She sits and waits
For words – all blather.

A letter comes.
Her fingers tremble.
A baby cries.
She smiles, dissembles.

The pocket watch
Has crazed its glass.
She slams the drawer:
The last, least straw.

The Pursuit

for Miroslav Holub

– What are you trying to re-capture inside yourself?
– My whole.
– Your hole?
– Yes, my whole.
– And what will be the duration of this seeking?
– As long as is required to define
　　　　the precise nature of the whole.
– But is not a hole a hole?
– Every whole is different, and mine
　　　　is more different than ever.
– But everyone recognises a hole when they see one.
　Its characteristics are self-evident.
– Only a fool would define the nature of the whole in that way.
– How then would you set *your* hole apart from the rest?
– Until I have found it, I cannot speak of its nature.
– Then how do you know what it is that you are seeking – and,
　indeed, whether there is anything at all to be sought in the
　first place that might even correspond to your *idea* of . . .
– Faint intimations.
– Intimations of a hole?
– Yes, intimations of the whole. Now you have it precisely.

The Exhibition

The loves that I have known are all displayed
Upon these trestle tables in the shade.
That white one has a pallor so serene –
No need to coax some complicating dream.
The black one, by the edge, still says she knows
What ruin means and where it sometimes goes.
But my best love's the blue, that marvellous head
With bird of clay on top. It pipes the dead
Back from the grave, into our arms again.
How can a cold thing give such warmth to men?

The Desolate Pilgrim

At length he reached a pool, some shriven place –
But not for him, embodiment of waste.
And so he turned, and beckoned to the night
That seemed to rise to an ungainly height.
The stars still peppered down, stinging his eye.
A thorn-bush menaced – like that friend who died.
It was imagined bliss, some scent of balm
That kept him plunging through the dark, unharmed.

History

History speaks confusedly, in dreams.
Black legs go marching – flies across a screen.
The icon waits. Its corner is obscure.
I pick about the leaf mould, seeking spoor.

Anemone

She was called, I think, Anemone.
I wouldn't say I knew her well –
Hardly at all.
She spoke, always, in an undertone.
She had grown very young again,
In a matter of months it seemed,
And very stooped and small.
She came to this door regularly.
She just stood there and waited –
For nothing at all.
I too waited,
On my side,
The inside,
For the fistfalls.
When it came, it was hard and brutal,
Three rough, rapid falls,
And then it stopped.
But if I didn't go
And talk to her,
Immediately open up my door,
She would wait out there for hours on end,
Not doing a thing, just breathing,
For a while, and then pretending to
Be something else – a dog or cat or something,
Anything with a small, insinuating call.
Anemone, I would say, speaking from the inside,
Please go away.
I need to do some work,
I cannot concentrate on anything at all
If you just stand out there and bawl.
I'm not bawling, she would say
In a normalish sort of voice,
I'm not talking even.
I'm just sitting, on this floor, out here,
Trying to be something sleek and thin
And even faintly beautiful.

The Look

Here is my face. I offer you its look –
Squint-eyed, dissembling, like some wintry rook.
If you should choose it, let me tell you now:
A look can change; a look is not a vow.
There are so many – and they're seldom true.
And as for that far-distant dream of *you*,
Composed of looks I caught across a room –
Who knows what they were meant for? Or for whom?
Were you to tell me, I would pick your words
To pieces, being a scavenger bird.

A maze of mazes

Lost in surprise, he draws a maze,
A maze of mazes, on the chair,
That perfect, gleaming nursery chair,
Where mother sat and combed his hair.

The hair fell out and he survived,
And kneels now, hugging at the chair,
And making scribbles, tracing lives,
The way they dance and dodge and dare.

This crayon is his *wunderkind*,
Clean azure blue and very smooth.
He twists it, twirls it, fingering
Its roundnesses, all through and through . . .

Quick glimpse of loss

Still overwhelmed by self-disgust,
He gained this measure of her trust –
The chance to catch her swinging free
From someone else's balcony,
Her body's loose and languid flow
Like all he'd known from long ago.

It was the best he could achieve –
He knew that, even as he heaved
Himself onto the windowsill,
And called to her, and swallowed pills.

On her eightieth birthday

These are the old rooms again,
So blank and so white,
And yet eternally renewing.
They dazzle my fancied sight.
Yet are these not the new rooms now?
The well-sprung floors vibrate
With the music of it all –
'The music of what?' you may ask.
Why, the music of all our futures
Still beyond recall.

Manifesto

Resist the temptation of rhyme.
Avoid the easy locution,
The steady rhythmical beat
Announcing, at some distance,
Where you must go and what take.
Step out of the door into inclement weather –
That cold snap again, with a hint of brick dust in the eye –
And stare across into the valley's bottom.
The smoke is lying low again. There is nothing to prize.

The Impingement of the Past

Old newspapers. A jug. One shelf of books.
Fond memories of hopeless, helpless looks.
Old limbs, odd faces staring out the night.
Teeth in a jar. Spent mysteries of light.

Expectancy

I live and die and live again
Beyond the slight esteem of men.

My speech is awkward, short my breath
When face to face with emptiness.

I cannot speak of love's release
Or other labours come to grief.

My shadow mocks me on the wall,
Still taunting that I live at all.

And yet I live. I cannot die
Until that last, slow, searching sigh

Removes me to some other place
Where all is emptiness and waste.

The March of the Colours

The colours are surging across the world.
Our hands are raised uselessly against them.
We shout: You are too vivid for our eyes!
They do not listen.
Without explanation or hesitation
Red is poured foaming into the blood,
Green washes its tide across the grasses,
And the sea, in its vain attempts to dodge, feint and weave,
Achieves a hopelessly mangled palette of greens, blues, and . . .
Things merely borrowed, willy-nilly, from fresh-painted leaves
and trees.

Observing the Queen of the Clouds

I say without a shadow of hesitation
That my adoptive mother is Queen of the Clouds,
And that Tassel, her bird, bears toward me no rancour.
It is not true that I have been here
As long as the idea of this painting has endured.
I was an afterthought, a touch of levity,
Some late modulation of mood –
Until I switched parts and came into myself.
What I desire above all things else
Is the phial of spices that she holds in her hand.
It is the key to my everything.
It will be all that I shall come to understand.
Pay no heed to Tassel. His thoughts are on that airy elsewhere
To which his ragged wings will bear him, upward, upward –
Like that phial on my dear mother's hand.
My eye rolls longingly. When will she notice?
She sees me here – and yet she does not heed.
Her mind is on that greater journey
When she will rise to shape that formlessness above
Into a kind of heavenly mead.

A Prayer at the Door

He asked to be nothing more
(the door was not a compromise)
Than perfect in himself
(the door was ever as before)
Ready, oh, willing to ablute
(provided, of course, there was a door)
And eager to step forth and out
(carefully closing the door)
To draw the pith from persons, things
(they do – or did – exist beyond the door)
Temper that loutish roar
(one's back to the door)
And, at evening's end, return
(behind the door)
Sleep through a knock of dreams
(the creaking door)
Awake, refreshed, ready to spring
(assault the door)
To carve his name
(again, upon the door)
Again again again
Upon the door.

Beside the Point

The dog was gaping with a special face.
The sticks were ranged in clusters by the wall.
The cock was walking tall amongst the hens.
The piled-up sky was ruminating rain.
My books were savaging the shelves they love.
My thinnish hands were contemplating grease.
My mother's foot was poking through the door.
I wondered if I loved the clothes I wore.
'But this is home . . .', the chant went, on and on,
Beside the point, I felt, 'and still my own . . .'.
I could not stem those words. They drove so strong,
Like breathless armies scything rights and wrongs.

There

That sudden, disruptive arrival
Of certain kinds of truth
And shadowy half-truths:
Some urgent sense of perspiration perhaps
On the balcony's outer edge,
His thumb pressed into
The rim of the wine glass,
The consequences travelling
Up to the wry smile and
Beyond the forehead –
He was about to give the world at large
At least half his attention.
These visionary moments,
He was thinking,
Blind one . . . to the
Momentary gleams,
The windowed expectations.
Her sudden, disruptive arrival,
Cat in hand,
The body working uneasily
Within the hand
Like a motor,
Caused him to stand back,
Take stock of
The truths of himself,
His awkward stance
Within this room
Awash with bloodless light . . .
Some man, attentive,
But behind,
Eagerly ready to step up
And out,
Pouring light, like
Tepid water,
Into the glass of himself,
Which was astir

Within his fingers,
Those shadowy,
Splashily tinkling
Tingles . . .

That which makes possible

Not only did he enable our fingers to find the pin.
He it was who fashioned the pin in the first place.
And now I see an angel standing on its head,
On the head of the pin, and that seems a marvel to me.

Not only did he enable our eyes to see the light.
He it was who fashioned the light in the first place,
Wrestling with it as if it were strong thews of dough
To be bent and twisted into shape, overlaying the firmament
As the pastry stretches across and overlays the baking tin.

Not only did he enable our bodies to use the force
With which nature had endowed us;
He it was who gave the body its electrical charge,
Willing it to hurtle through seas, scarify land,
Raising sparks and dust,
And fall then in a whispered, twisting heap.

Sweet Balm of Hellebore

A fire was spitting in a room.
The flower had not attained full bloom.
A man was sitting in the hearth,
Wearing a hat, maybe a scarf.

The wind was rattling the blinds.
Some cat was mewing to its kind.
He seized the hat and threw it in the fire.
That is the end, he said, of all desire.

The rain came on. It beat down on the roof.
The portrait of his mother stared, aloof.
He took the scarf and wound it round his wrist.
He beat the ground with it, saying: that fish

That I just ate has made me sick.
My guts are raw. If I could only wish
For one phylactery from my father's store,
I *know* what it would be:
Sweet balm of hellebore.

Somewhere

The bell is lying heavy on my heart.
I don't want to start.

The ocean comes and goes inside my head.
Would I were there instead.

A garden in the midst of a field
Seems a little unreal.

My mother's tongue is red
From prattling all day long about the dead.

Morality

The stars are raging in their nests,
But Man, tall in his shoes,
Seems to know best.

The birds are screaming
Up and down the wires.
My bed is cold.
Some man came in,
Put out the fire.

The fire, as I recall,
Spat in a room
That looked like this one.
Some woman came and went
Before the man was even dreamt.
She left too soon.

The body's broken biscuit
Tastes like wood.
The dog that sniffed it
Came to no good.

The stars are raging in their nests,
But Man, tall in his shoes,
Seems to know best.

An Arranged Meeting

Passing through rooms, we come at last
To corridors, prickly with damp heat,
And then to other rooms again,
And, last, a garden where we meet,

Quite awkwardly at first, and then
He smiles and tells me to my face
It wasn't what he'd wanted, no,
This meeting in this other place.

What he'd imagined was a home
Or something like, with books, a view
Of kiddies laughing till they scream,
And us inside, us, laughing too . . .

Confusionism

Stare at birds' legs on fragments of papyrus
Until, giggling, you begin to approach
The condition of the ecstatically blind.
Breathe deeply, slowly at first, taking in
Larger and larger gulps of air
Until your whole being
Is flooded with oxygen.
Now begin to thrash your arms about in the air
As if conducting Mahlerian orchestras
At all points of the compass.
If your feet do not rise from the ground
Of their own accord,
Check carefully whether you have indeed divested yourself
Of all items of dress.
Did a tie, for example, remain in place
For reasons of false modesty?
Wrench off that tie!
No such ties are recognised – let alone flaunted –
Within the spiritual kingdom of Confusionism.
That done, come together as one
And establish the perfect commonwealth
Of free and unaligned spirits.

The Relinquishment of Responsibility

All can be transformed by dint of sheer hard work –
Consider this face, for example, its taut, anxious grimaces,
That small, petulant mouth with its labouring speech,
Those fiercely insinuating hands, twisting and turning purseward,
and,
Worst, the steaming bulk of the body itself as it leers and
leans . . .
Wrench each thing off, plunge back into the vat.
Let the forgeress try her hand to get it pat.

The Meaning of the Lost Piece of Music

'Il faudrait pouvoir réentendre cette pièce que personne ne joue.' *Les Cormorans*, Philippe Jacottet, p. 58

'The problem with music, of course, is that it means precisely nothing.' Anthony Burgess

Listen, once again, to this piece of music that no one plays.
Hear, now, as I rehearse it in my mind's coolest ante-room,
Fiddling as slowly and fastidiously as I am able,
Back turned stolidly to that blaze of light at the window.
It begins with a movement as furtive as the gesture
Of a wrist half-turned upon a table,
Marking the futile beginnings of some soon-to-be-aborted
assignation.
A mere six bars later you hear the ghost of some lost – though
not wholly so –
Passion begin to stir: the god is waking up,
Having churned twice in his sleep, after that deepest embrace
Of an absent pillow.
He knows, already, how much of this world
There is to be observed,
And where to begin –
What finger end, for example, to lick for the wind's direction.
He rises now – and then it all falls away,
Suddenly, lamentably far,
Into an abyss of some kind, would you say?
Too much rumour and shadow.
Too much breathy rumour. Too many heavy hints of shadow . . .
Before, all of a sudden,
We burst up and out into the snow.
It is winter and, yes, the world is
Scintillatingly dead to all footfalls . . .
Of music, that is as much as one ever needs to know.

The Smoker's Reverie

The mother's here. I watch her cry.
And then time does the strangest thing.
It sucks the tears back to her eyes.
It burnishes that dull gold ring.

A man appears, unknown to me,
Who speaks in lulling, whispered words.
She disappears into the street.
A motor coughs. Cries go unheard.

And now a girl runs in, flushed, dumb.
Though tall as me, she's wiry thin.
Our fingers touch . . . A baby thumb
Is proffered, so I put it in.

I draw on absence, leaning here,
Beside a chair that doesn't change.
A chair will stare at windows, walls
As past and future dream and range.

The Ascent

To that camp on the hill he bore up
The most perfect of civilising odours,
Together with a jiggle of
Bright-shining artefacts
By which he might
Memorialise himself:
Musk, trapped in a fluted jar,
Of the sleek cats he had slain;
Tusks of the wild boar,
Pared to a point of perfection;
And the green, hollow-eyed stare
Of a mask of lichened bark
Which would, he avowed,
Allow him to see
In the darkest and most uncivil of darks.

Thus encumbered, he made his way
At the mid point of the day,
Whistling, beneath his breath,
Tunes which assumed,
In that high, thin air,
The brilliantly mannered shapes
Of Celtic runes.
How long ago did all this happen?
You may well ask.
Why, only yesterday, I say –
Though what day it is today
Would be altogether trickier to grasp.

The Grief of Mothers

It's Winter now. The peace keepers are here.
Their flags are idling in the slack-jawed wind.
Nikolic swears he'll tame them with a vow.
What use are *you* to anyone? He grins.
I am a mother – seventeen times over.
I know the grief of mothers in this world.
I know the way our arms rise, wave and fall.
Beneath these drifts of snow, my flag lies furled.

The sure penetration of black

This man, this ecclesiastical grandee of a man, was once my
bosom friend.
See how he sweeps, with a practised flourish of black, into the
room,
And takes his seat as if the seat already belonged to him.
Listen to the resounding tinkle of his people's voice,
A voice accustomed to the caressing amplifications of the
microphone.
Only his body falls short a little of that voice:
Stooped now, with a sad, drooping paunch, the cassock
Does its levelling best to contain what he has snatched and
plundered
By way of rest from the ceaseless need to be
That man whom all men love in their own poor stead.

The Luminescence of the Poem

This poem is possessed of its own tender blue light
Whose radiant warmth will shield us from all harm
When the voices of dissent appear, locked arm to arm.
The poem's brave architecture, smooth, tall,
            and conically shrewd,
Pleasing beyond the threshold of sanity,
Will offer a pool-like interlude,
Transforming this room, with its dull and shabby mien,
The mock-anguish of these dog-eared tomes,
Into an airy temple of purity and light
By means of the perplexing simplicity
Of a mild, tender, poem-blue light.

The geographical location of the poem

The refugees, mired in mud all day,
Glimpsed a poem at the end of the hill's beaten track
From which they ate and drank. Relaxed,
They slept and dreamt of storms,
Storm-clouds, quick fires, and a small dog's rage.
Then the dream turned the page.
When they awoke, there they were still,
Where the poem had left them,
Chilled on the side of the hill.
But below stretched an abundant plain
Of a broadly uncomplicated green.
The poem chuckled past
Like an underground stream.

The merest sliver of balm

The furthest corner of the human eye
Is the supreme seeing instrument.
Look ahead and all you catch
Is chaos heaped upon chaos, filth upon filth.
Look sidewise, as if through the curtain's chink,
And you have it all,
All that there is to see and to know
Of earthly nobility.
Not much, granted, but just enough
To prevent you, all night,
Twisting and twisting about in the bed,
And screaming, endlessly, through your
Huge, wide-open, cyclopean eye . . .
Dive into it then, arms by your sides,
If you find yourself small enough
To approach its mysteries,
But, first, take three whole lungsful of breath
And remain ever watchful lest,
Unawares, you catch your death.

The Painter

'Rills of oily eloquence . . . lubricate the course they take.'

William Cowper

The wind-whipped silver hair,
Paint-clotted thumbs,
An easel, wildly angled from the true,
A gulley, strait, in shadow,
Where he peers,
The painter
Who is not the likes of you.

No, not the likes of you –
Some other kind,
A finer thing, more sensitive and still
In his slow contemplation
Of a scene
That narrows
To the snakiest of rills.

The snakiest of rills
Is what he seeks,
Some image of it, devious as thought,
An almost human motion
Bodied forth
In pigments
Mixed and matched and overwrought.

Adjoining worlds

When you repeat these experiences of ours –
That simple trick of going abroad, for example –
You make them sound like fantastical tales
Of lives lived in some glorious Otherwhere
By beings lovelier and better-favoured
By far than ourselves. Whose mistake is it then?
Mine, to suppose us humdrum and ordinary
No matter how glittering the sea?
Or yours, to proclaim us different from ourselves,
Wholly transmogrified by sun and light's mystery?

Death's fond histrionics

To be resurrected with the dead
Is to be disgusted by the sight of
Old limbs whirling and weaving
Between the stars
As if they partook of
The glitter of youth again.
See how their rags of flesh
Come fluttering down
Through the sky like leaves!
Can they not see
That there is no pleasure
To be gained from this display?
Can they not act their age?

To Browning

Robert Browning, you were a man
Who knew the brief company
Of a saintly wife
Whose verses were your equal,
And whose life was blameless –
Upright, strong to fight
The cause of women
In an age of toppered men
Whose measure was your wisdom,
Mouthing philosophies
Beyond their ken.

The Mouse in the Statue

Where the god once lived,
There sleeps a mouse
Secure inside
A tiny house
Of sawdust, sand and beetle dung . . .
His life there just goes on and on,
Serene and safe
From cats and snakes
While priests patrol
The temple gates.

When the people come,
They worship still,
Not knowing that
Their god is ill . . .
A mouse, eating its heart away,
Will bring it down to earth one day
And, once laid low,
It will not know
To resurrect
Itself – and go . . .

Death of a Poet

Lorca is here. I flesh him with my flesh.
I dream the burden of his loveless nights.
I watch him die – such ignominious rest
For one so free, abandoned in his flights . . .

Lorca is here. The gypsy in his bed
Has packed the song away and left for good.
The tune still lingers, dribbling from my head
Like Cana's water, scenting wine or blood . . .

At Lac Léman

A large and near fatal gathering of opportunities,
Which takes in public opprobrium, private grief,
and a curiously beguiling medley – or was it a melody? –
        of in-betweens;
And all this in the context of a lake whose like
He had never before seen –
A straggle of bathers (largely grosser kine),
And an imprint of ducks' feet between the pebbles,
Where a string's course of wet sand
Had made itself repeatedly available.

The Clergyman's Daughter

A woman in a room who suffers pain,
My mother, or some other's, rocking there
With nothing else to think of or prepare,
No human to live up to. He's elsewhere.

A woman, an old woman, crying now,
Seeing a blankness stretching out ahead,
The blankness of non-being, reaching out
From shore to shore to shore inside her head.

An old, fat woman squatting by a fire
Within a room that's bounded by small rooms,
Having no living impulse, no desire
To shift from here at all, or to resume

That search for father's other better place
Where once he thought serenity might be.
These thoughts of him gust in. She sees his face,
And then it flickers, dies, beside her knees.

The song's gradual awakening

The favours hung from branches, by the sea.
The house was leaning awkwardly, all night.
Some central plank was missing. Let it be.
The favours spun and frolicked in the light.

That empty car looked jagged – at the edge.
The bleeding finger hadn't yet been sewn.
It's not quite what I want, that solemn pledge,
The cage said. Let's pretend the bird has flown.

The minstrels' convocation? One whole day
Of weary strum-, strum-, strumming in the heat.
I'm tired of it all now, though others say
It brought a different nation to its feet.

The deceiving texture of fresh-faced blooms

The rain comes on. The rain comes on too soon.
It washes all the faces in the street.
It freshens up the flowers until they bloom
Like plastic ones inside a room on heat –

This room in which my mother sits and dreams,
Staring at flowers melting in the heat,
That slow drip drip of plastic on the clean
White floor she washed with her own tears this week . . .

But they're not real, I tell her, can't you see?
Are you that blind? Can't your old fingers feel
How plastic feels, that strange consistency
When heat has melted it, like jellied eels?

She knows – and yet she knows not – what she knows.
I drag her from the chair and out the door.
I point to how the rain streams down. I show
Her shredded petals, flower heads – bald, bald, bald.

The Poem Factory

This is a poem factory. Do not enter.
The noxious stench of gases will clear
When the product emerges,
Colourless, pristine and definitive,
In the fullness of time future.
The wheezes and the groans that you hear
Are necessary stages in the difficult and painful business
Of poetical gestation.
Poems are not deposited at regular intervals.
Some are small-scale projects, fashioned of themselves;
Others, in scope and ambition, are looser-limbed
And swingeingly Wagnerian.
It is not possible to reserve a poem
For your particular pleasure.
We do not also embellish greetings cards.
Money, proffered in advance, is quite useless.
We do not recognise its value
Until we are about to starve.
We, the workers, are lean, feverish, stick-like beings
Who know, above all, what is at stake.
Being antennae – *your* antennae – we *boing*
At a furious and well nigh incalculable rate.

Gradual Dissolution

She dies a little every single day.
I watch her fade – the eyes, the teeth, the nails . . .
Those eyes . . . a film develops like a mist.
The teeth – a whiteness edging off to grey . . .

I love her and *I'd* rather die instead.
My death would be . . . well . . . quite another thing,
Some gorgeous cavalcade, a trump on high,
Four angels bearing up my baldaquin.

And I, in marble, palm to sweatless palm,
Eyes closed serenely, locked against the day,
That day when I shall rise in paradise,
Without a body, brain or mind to stray . . .

The Human Predicament

A meagre shaft of sunlight pierced the cage
In which the human animal lay splayed,
And tickled at one ear, which twitched, annoyed
To be maltreated like some childhood toy.

It fell asleep again, for half a year,
And dreamt of sunlight tickling that ear.
It rose up in a rage – and then it saw
The sun's yolk spilled across the stinking floor.

It tried to lap it up – it had no food –
But all it got was filth upon the tongue.
It huddled in a corner, mute, confused.
The sun's aurora teased it like a song.

In Pursuit of the Poem

Houses lost in a landscape.
Houses buried at the ends of rutted lanes.
Houses, with rooms and rafters exposed
To the workings of the elements.
Houses, no longer regarded as habitations at all,
But rather the coarse materials from which houses were once fashioned,
Strewn everywhere, as if nothing and no one mattered.
And the humans, for whom these houses represented a home,
Lost and scattered too, as if nothing mattered to them,
And no one cared where they, the scattered remnants
Of fragile human communities,
Fell, in bits and pieces, by the wayside,
Trodden underfoot, with the shards of their belongings
Worked and turned by the elements
Into the stuff of lanes long rutted
At the lost ends of landscapes.

Personal Ad

Modest grass landscape
For hard old battered black suitcase.
Landscape misused by rain, hail, feet and snow.
Suitcase mangled battered and torn
By feet fingers rain hail and snow.
Modest slouched battered black body
In hard old grass landscape
Misused by what has misused
Hard old battered black suitcase
And modest grass landscape:
Rain, hail, feet, fingers and snow.

Swooning in the factitious element

These are the finer fruits of self-regard:
Poems addressed to the self, as if the self
Were some species of immortal being
Requiring the worshipful attention of its grateful subjects
In the daylight hours and evening.

These are the finer fruits of self-regard:
A truly majestic display of other people's poems,
In book and pamphlet form,
So that likeness will be forever gazing upon likeness,
And thereby creating some pervasive sense of inner calm.

If these finer fruits should suddenly be absent –
Poems no longer written, books burnt or lost –
Watch him stream out of the doorway,
And plunge, crazed, ragless, storm-tossed,
Straight into the arms of old drinking cronies
In whose faces we pray he may read:
Long poems of self-regard,
Whole tomes of perfectly patterned imagined lives.

The Blue String Vest

I own my life.
I clasp it to myself.
It's all I have.
There's really nothing else.
The women come.
They peer into my eye.
I look elsewhere.
I wish they wouldn't pry –
Or even try
To steal my flesh.
I tear so easily –
Just like this blue string vest.

The House of Miniatures

I coax my little people into life.
I feed the flames that flicker in their eyes.
I lead them by the hand, up to the door.
I teach them how to say it: gentles, more . . .

I cherish all that smallness – tiny lips
With which to plant a steady wooden kiss;
And hips, secured by nails, from which to vow
Eternal fealty – with a stiff bow.

The Rehearsal

The Great Theatre of Public Grief is everywhere!
Men, gloriously spread-eagled on the ground like famous tragedians,
Lips puffed up, still trickling word-shapes red with fury;
Women, old ones, young ones too, repeatedly clutching at,
And then tossing away, their handkerchiefs –
Such genuine perfectionists!
Children, stumping, wailing, this way, that way,
Up and down the crazed, soft-lit streets,
Comical as decapitated chickens . . .
And those doctors – posed against that plain, hospital-like façade –
In their off-white gowns,
Still – still! – weeping over the absence of empty needles . . .
Yes, this great theatre of grief is everywhere.
Capture it quickly before the sun,
That fatal optimist,
Burns out the eye of your prying lens.

Beauty and Sausages

The loss of beauty, to our future lives,
Will mean as much as sausage meant today.
The loss of sausage taste on eager tongues
Will not prevent the time slipping away.

The memory of sausage will soon fade,
The fatness and the grease that oozed around,
The ripping of those tender, crisped up skins,
That sense of pleasure as the bits went down.

The memory of beauty will soon fade,
The overwhelming rightness of it all,
Will be replaced by other rightnesses, amongst
Which misery and death will walk quite tall.

A Fisherboy trapped in the Manor House in Winter

These measureless, cold rooms
Bring back to me
The way I have been
Tempered by the sea.

The chill, the slap of boards,
That faint horizon line –
It seems almost a ship
Drowned in the countryside.

And if I were to run
And clear the sill,
A wave would catch me
In its quick, cold thrill.

The Concrete Walkway

I knew a concrete walkway, out at sea.
The people passed along with slow, bowed heads.
The rubbish seemed of little consequence.
The seagulls snatched away the chicken legs.

I knew a concrete walkway, hard and cold,
And colder still when winter stamped its foot,
And bristled, dagger-like, with icicles.
But nothing made those searching eyes glance up.

Each one continued to regard his feet
In spite of all the spectacle out there –
Those grey, frizzed waves, the unexpected leap
Of strangers who, all costs assessed, had dared.

What did we do when night slammed shut its book?
What did we do when dawn, spread-eagled, yawned?
What did we do with noon-tide's searing look?
What did we do when evening stooped to warn?

I knew a concrete walkway, out at sea.
The people passed along with slow, bowed heads.
The rubbish seemed of little consequence.
The seagulls snatched away the chicken legs.

Lady Mary Wortley Montagu's Epistle to Mr Pope

You ask me, Mr Pope,
What it is exactly that I feel now, being dead,
And lodged here in these Elysian Fields,
With the Black Sea beneath me,
And the fountains playing about my heels.
I feel serene, safe and beyond the call
Of the world's manifold impertinences – yes, that above all –
No longer wishing to arbitrate
Between the red shift and the gold,
Or become impassioned over
Those interminable games of piquet of old.
I wish you well with your labours
Down there in those filthy London streets,
And, did I not feel its opposite,
I might even say to you: let us meet . . .

Old Blues Lyric

Sweet Jesus laid him down
On an ample feather bed.

He surely was a tired boy now
On account of the blood he had shed.

I didn't think one thing
To the stain that he left on my sheet.

They say that man's blood does endure.
And I say that Jesus is sweet.

Sweet is a funny old word
That means nothing, but something to me.

Sweet was the kiss that I gave.
And sweet was the kiss he gave me.

But was he alive when he kissed?
And was it a real thing I felt?

And am I alive to tell this?
Or is this a holler from hell?

My Girl Rwanda

My girl Rwanda,
Squatted by the fire,
Tossing in the little logs,
Make the flames go higher.

Where has mummy gone today?
Where has daddy been?
Why's he sitting in the dark,
Hand propping his chin?

Soon it will be night again.
Soon the goat man come
With a tinkle of his bell.
Then the children run.

But we don't run out today.
Daddy say: stay in!
Be no goat man hereabout.
Storm is rolling in.

But there is no black up there.
Neither sound of rain.
Blueness, blueness all the day,
Sunlight, plain as plain.

Still he say: don't you go out.
You just build the fire.
So I squat me here and watch
Flames go jumping higher.

Now the water steaming hard,
Water in the tub
Squatting on the flaming fire.
Soon I rub and rub.

Daddy, bring the kangas here.
Toss them in the tub.
Rwanda wash the stains away.
See me rub and scrub.

Poetry in Performance

I present myself.
And now I'm here.

My head shines forth –
So bald and clear.

The platform's high.
Hot lights make blind.

I choose my voice.
It lags behind.

I tell it: forward,
Strut your piece!

Its faint, far croak says:
Cornish geese . . .

The Fire Grate

The furthest corners of a man's pent disposition
Are filled with the stench of imperfect half-thinkings –
The means to achieve, as yet uninvestigated
With the thoroughness they scarcely deserve;
The futile habits of failure, perfectly balanced and oiled,
And available for use at any given moment of a sultry noon-tide.
And all this, if desired, may be bunched up into a very small
space
Until it resembles something akin to a fistful of crumpled
newspaper –
Certainly fit enough to stuff another man's small and indifferent
fire grate.

Coming Upon That Moment of Anticipation

He waits and waits for things to happen,
But when they happen, who is there

To see them flaring in his doorway,
A foot or two beneath his stare?

The best that may be hoped is stillness
In which to count the words that fall

From voices jostling in that doorway,
Which soon recede to inner halls.

The Attenuated Violinist from Mitteleuropa

Having passed through the small death of sleep,
He awoke to the larger and more gradual death of waking.
Where was he now? Potsdam still? Or somewhere else?
He groped for his trousers, but found only legs,
And what pitiful things they seemed to be,
No more substantial than the bow
Of his beautiful violin that hung from the wall.
They had taken his violin one night
And beaten its heart out against the stones.
How he had wept to see it happen.
They had not even allowed him
To gather up the fragments from the ground.
Now, when no one is looking,
He sleeps with the precious bow in his arms –
Two stringy lovers, dreaming of Potsdam perhaps,
Or of strolling, some balmy evening,
Across the ornamental gardens,
And listening to the faint, sweet quailing
Of the grace notes of some distant violin.
Could it be his cousin's perhaps –
She whom he would never after meet?

II

French Manners

Fashioning Beginnings

The fine dew made a promise to the grasses and the stones.
The heat of our countryside stood outside, yawning.
The implements of work had yet to be awakened.
A couple by Giacometti, thin-strung, were poised to choose
the close path.
Their wishes, feverish, hung on the air for cocks to observe,
Fresh from that raucous farmyard.
Naked or not, the couple hastened,
Having some destiny to unravel or pursue.
The church windows were burning behind the deep, forbidding
plunge of the well.
There was passion in the pricking thistle, but none at
the house core.
Giacometti was sleeping in what we all called the rustic chamber.
Oh, to be, for once in one's life, rid of this illness of the self,
He was thinking, as he spun on his axis
Like the roller of some new-fangled printing machine,
Clanking, and squeezing out its gel.
And then his dog struck up, putting an end to such
mental fatuity.
And he rose on his elbow, with a face, or faces, still to fashion . . .

Impossible Horizons

I go in pursuit of impossible horizons.
Day closes in – and that is all there is.
Night is no more a resting place than death itself.
See this mirror. I walk into it one day – and then the next . . .
A ghost sits here pulling ridiculous faces.
I know who she is. She speaks my name everywhere,
Calling me Little Orphan of the Raspberries.
She has plucked them already, she says. But from where?
Someday I shall catch all this quick life in a net.
No slippery thing will be too small for my mesh.
But today I see everything to be impossible.
Today I am gorged on too much cerebration . . .
If anyone speaks of me, calls me friend to my own,
Let them babble like babies, going on and on.
This present is so murky now. New wars are coming –
Year after year, each with its forgettable name.
I cannot forgive man his bloodlust, that aching for
Strife at all cost, that so eager whetting of blades.
Jean-Paul is my son. I call him such.
Speech is his portion. The body is wrenched from its pole.
Every day I visit him. Each noontide sees me walking.
When I find the inside of him, when I tear at his root,
Then you will know. For there will surely be aching.

Objet Trouvé Chez René

The spur of day and the wall of night.
And the two linked together
By the beads of a man's spittle.
The fields are swept bare again.
We are too poor to claim them.
The colours strung out on the sky
Are not dripping.
We stare into the blank spaces
For some hint of an orchestra.
The bassoon that hangs there in the clouds
Is, alas, only cloud.
The cloud that hangs in the sky
Is, alas, only sky
Let us pluck the bassoon and play it
As if we were alone.

Vapours

It was a confident winter,
With man his own huntsman,
And yet, there we were, all at sea
In the Alps of Provence.
The woman who was sharing our weather
Each morning bent over our papers
And snickered.
We told her we painted with love,
Passion, abandon.
She seemed not to look at
The bulbous fruits of our patience.
She seemed to care for nothing,
No detail at all but our stinking clothes
Piled up higher and darker than hills
In the corner.
My friend is a poet, I said,
Raking his hair with my fingers.
And then out fell the louse.
Or did it just jump, jump for joy
From the end of my finger?
I have, this moment, to thank you,
Ciska Grillet, I told him,
Ignoring entirely her turbulence.
Our concern must be with ourselves.
Art, to be sure, to be tangy,
Must open its mouth
To the juice of the fruits . . . of the kingdom.
It must dream in the mountains, the meadows . . .
She seemed not to hear,
Standing there like a pillar of reason,
Poised to fall and to crush us.

The Newest Constellation

My Balzac lies there, prone across his sky.
Join up the winking dots – regard his corporality!
He was a slob. He wrote all day and night.
His hair was greasy-lank, fake title social-bright.
His carrot fingers soaked up blots of ink.
He wrote more novels than mere man could dream or think.
He lived in fear – the money came and went.
His debtors howled like wolves outside the tenements.
He was a stinking monster – just like me
And all the rest of this so human comedy
That sluices through the sewers of Passy
Toward Death's drowning sea . . .

Paris 1945

It was Picasso who stood alone at the gate
To the infernal regions, barring their way to us.
It was Picasso, the master carpenter,
Who fashioned the thousand tools of our future peace.
It was Picasso who shed his moonlight upon this darkened world,
And set his Minotaur at the heels of the unwary.
It was Picasso who, in the month of July
Of the year 1939, amidst the dread hypnosis
Of this perjured capital,
Taught us to bask in our shadows
And take up once more the communal life.

L'Académie Française

Racine is setting fire to our hearts
With a box containing
Forty-eight precisely fashioned
Spent matches.
Corneille is sitting for his laurel crown.
Each time he tries it on,
It seems too small.
Rousseau, giggling, trouserless,
Is at the dancing school,
Teaching the little girls.
Rimbaud is urging his fleas
To jump higher than
The flames of paradise.
Diderot is panting heavily
Up the stairs,
Bearing the book of books
Upon his head.
Gravitas is in his tread.
Balzac is crawling at speed
Through the sewers of Passy,
Debtors howling at his back.
He strikes a match – and then another.
Damp *alors*!
He searches his pockets.
Somewhere, he knows, there is a map
That points the way
To the Académie . . .

A Surrealist Lost in the Himalayas

These snow-driven summits have no hands.
They consist of nothing but
White, sleeveless tents.
No sooner do I pack
One blizzard away into a box
Of such and such dimensions
Than it springs out again,
Whirling around
This question mark
Like the shreds of some ghostly patrimony
Spitting out its taunts.
The black wives are massed at the base camp.
Even from this distance
I recognise their doleful hum.
And now the telephones are squawking like ravens
Strung out on tenuous wires,
Slopes are raining blunt knives of ice . . .
Oh, I must caution the witness approaching
Lest he jam open too soon
The breathless door to this life.

Récit

Apprehension, I say, is no less rich than hope.
It contains the day and the night of tomorrow, and succeeding tomorrows;
But the night that waits to seize upon its twilight
Is longer and more perilous by far than the day,
Which can scarcely be said to be wished for.
And this is why our epoch,
Which no longer assigns to this earth,
Or to the beings that flit across it,
Death as a natural, healing consequence of life,
Recognises and accepts it
Like some abrupt, instantaneous interruption,
No matter when, no matter where;
A species of fatality that is
The predictable and wished for consequence of error,
Arising from the clumsiness of gods and men.
If one were able to foresee all this,
Creation would lack efficacity, and beauty
Would be incapable
Of teaching us a lesson.
Let us therefore have the courage and the equipoise
Not to fall to our knees too readily,
Nor to renounce our future,
No matter how much we may live in fear of it.
This chaos in the arts will pass away
Like every chaos heretofore.
And those who survive
Will be those who have enriched their deaths
By experience, which means
The proper incubation of one's natural resources.
Ghika is amongst those whom
I would wish to name.
His work will stand proud,
Outfacing the mirror's glory.
His expansive measure,
According to my predictions,

Will never lose its way.
He comes to us, fleet-footed, from afar,
Settling upon the windows of morning,
Bearing in his arms
That Grecian world of earth and
Improvisatory knowledge.
Earth, from which we must never be separated!
Let us glut ourselves upon it
Until our bodies and our minds are sated.
O Eupalinos, mewling Pythian infant,
It is Ghika alone who will drain you
Of your tragic vision of yourself.
O second Nietzsche that you are –
Nietzsche, Nature, Nurture . . . –
Puff out your cheeks
And blow the sails of Telemache of old,
And let us never say, even amongst ourselves,
That we have known the end of things today!

(*after the French of René Char*)

Impressionistic Marvels

The exactitudes of Spring have long since passed away –
Thanks to Monet, that old buffoon who creaks along his gravel
path,
Burdened with riches – like an ass.
Today I applied two fresh water lilies
To my burning eyes.
You would be surprised how it affected –
For better or for worse, needless to say –
The trenchancy of my vision,
These colours God has set before my eyes.

Perhaps One Would Have Spoken Thus In The Presence of Braque . . .

When the snow is sleeping, night rises up and whistles to the dogs. O fruit, you reach out so far from your stems that the very stars in the sky seem to be your reflections!

We are lost when the line bends to the right. It is forever hurrying ahead of us, and even as we watch it becomes the ground on which we tread. And then we kneel before these stones of matchless felicity.

The savour of waves that hesitate to fall: they have no time for the sea's rising past.

It is in the feathers of the arrow that the blood lingers, not at all at its tip. The bow has ever wished it so.

The storm owns two houses. The first is less substantial than the grass blade. The second . . . well . . . even man himself would be hard pressed to encompass it.

The dew has suffered overmuch. At morning it broods upon the sweats of night; the children of day play too rough for its taste; but the worst by far is to stumble upon the ceaseless tumult of fountains.

Look! This man here is covered with bites. He has fallen victim to his imagination – whereas the imagination itself bleeds at the sight of the old wounds.

The end of art is a road which declines to a path, and at the path's end we seem to recognise some opening into a field . . . Yes, perhaps it is our birthright.

The Death of Blanchot

Blanchot threw his confidences to the winds.
He trusted no man or woman on this earth
Not to blather.
On the night of the eighteenth he was alone,
Weighing the value of his active life
Beside a sputtering fire.
The first man spoke his name.
The third one fired.
The other two fell to their knees – in shame,
According to the widow.
When news reached her,
Sped across the Seine by horse,
She fainted in the arms
Of her sister's son
(They were quite close,
according to the brother) –
Then took another.
The likeness of the monument
I cannot judge.
But some have said:
What life is there in stone
That does not budge?

Painterly Absorption

In the wordly department of painting
Where men may move with ease and pare their nails,
Picasso squats on his stool and, lifting down some basin,
Foliates it according to his taste.
A woman standing by feels for her hair.
No part of her is safe from that impish stare.

Execution in Monochrome

Every night of our lives some star is dying of thirst.
Even the picture books of our children,
Conceived in colours brilliant as the peacock's,
Have retired into a sullen monochrome.
And how monotonous our speech has become –
Especially when we are alone.
Words, once so various and mellifluous,
Fall wearily to the ground
Off the edges of our wasted lips.
The three or four who had walked together from their schooldays
Are now joined at the head.
If I were to write you a letter in order to explain all this,
You would marvel at the angle of my script . . .

Poet & Painter

The Painter

Take this garden chair, for example.
You will be agreeably surprised.
Now sit down.
Let me carry light into the studio.
It is time to throw water on these colours.
Here, orange stains, and there, beside it,
A plate. It is not colour alone, of course,
That smooths these thighs.
I come bearing joy in my wake.
What else is to be expected of the new?

The Poet

Your least actions have a familiar savour,
And the things that bask in the climate of your life –
They too preserve a certain attitude of truth,
Be that important or not.
So how *do* you make what you make?
To the eye they aspire to nothing more than
Companionship with yourself – thanks to your
Timely and propitious interventions.
Others have been known to caress
Too brutishly by far.

The Poet

This flagon has the crepuscular air
Of a working man who, having spent himself to the utmost,
Prepares to topple sideways into his bed . . .
I return to this matter of savour.
Your motives excite me – and yet they mask the eye
That observes them. No, blinking is not my excuse.
I shall not have recourse to the subterfuge
Of the gymnast.
And my jubilation, let it be known,
Is massive in its intensity.

You are a mass, a granite mass, of unspoken
and unrevealed possibilities.
There is life in here such as the grain shall know.
And your resistance is such that no accident
Will ever penetrate you to the quick.

The Painter

These ideas, you know . . . If I seem to step
Heavily amongst things, it is not,
For sure, in order to impoverish or,
Worse, exaggerate their singularity.
I climb as high as their nights.
I enter their first nudities. I give them
A craving for light everlasting, a
Curiosity for shadow, an avid
Wish to build and build. What matters
Is the foundation of new love amidst
Beings and things that have hitherto
Shown a truly withering
And magisterial degree of indifference.

Parallel Text: La Suisse Romande
Texte Parallèle: French Switzerland

C'est un jour calme de soleil dans l'histoire de la psychiatrie
suisse . . .
It is a calm summer's day in the history of Swiss psychiatry

Et les façons divers de penser – analytiques, philosophiques,
philologiques, phénoménologiques . . .
And the various modes of thought – analytical, philosophical,
philological, phenomenological

Sont aux abois. Se trouvent, en famille, à la plage souriante de
Lutry . . .
Are at bay. Are at the bay.

La Suisse imaginaire, c'est un pays de chèvres aux cloches
frêles . . .
My Switzerland of the mind is a country of goats, bells gently
tinkling

La Suisse actuelle, c'est un pays de grandes églises protestantes
aux cloches murgissantes
C'est une église de grands protestants, temples vivants, cloches
aux cous
C'est un pays de grosses banques et de gros banquiers
C'est un pays de mille champignons
– mélange de cent grammes: 4 francs
Tout disparaît au coeur de La Suisse –
La réalité des choses, la réalité
de l'argent étranger . . .
The real Switzerland is another matter altogether

La sortie de secours est bloquée inexplicablement
par une espagnole indifférente . . .
There is, however, no way out

'Explicit Software Parental Advisory'

A single T-shirt a prix réduite does not constitute a summer

Merci de votre confiance, messieurs, dames . . .
Thank you for your custom, gentlefolk
Mais non, monsieur, sank you for *your* customs

Moi, je n'ai rien à te déclarer, ma Suisse, ma soeur . . .
Sisters of Mercy,
Descended from the Alpine snows,
St Bernard-like
On grosses pattes they gos.

C'est un jour calme et orageux dans l'histoire du psychiatre suisse
It was a dark and stormy night within the cerebral context of the
Swiss psychiatrist

Il chicane . . .
His ovoid head pulsed with laughter

. . . et part pour les Cévennes
Next year – perhaps a gîte in the Cévennes . . .

Picasso and the Reich

Had they incarcerated the man,
Any illusion of normality
Would have been lost to view.
Had they shot or bludgeoned the man to death,
A mere painter, short, Spanish, lascivious,
Though possessed of a brilliant eye and hand,
Would have suffered the apotheosis
Of instant martyrdom.
So better by far to let him be,
Leave him free to work in that studio of his –
Arrondissement Seize –
On those portraits of women in profile
With both eyes on the same side of the face –
A mark, perhaps, of especial vigilance
In those difficult days.

An Ancient Antagonism

Voltaire is dead
And locked into his grave.
He will not rise,
Having eschewed
The trumps of paradise.

I light a candle,
Watch it dwindle down.
This smoke is equal to
His genius now.

Enter: the Acrobats of Night

(after Philippe Jaccottet)

Day draws back to the very extremities of earth
With the smooth and silent flourish
Of curtains in the opera house.

What are those puppets swinging up there
From the tallest rungs of the air?
They are the invisible stars
Pirouetting above our heads,
So clean and so bare.

And so it is that we live in these worlds
Of movement and distance,
While the mind, that long and cool parquet floor,
Keeps on gleaming,
Recedingly gleaming and gleaming . . .

The Concierge: a low note of lamentation

The concierge, lost in her own small courtyard,
Has not the wherewithal to mount the stairs.
Let the dust motes gather. Let the ghosts still linger.
Let it all break up and dissolve in air.

The concierge, circling her own poor hovel,
Spies a visitor hasten – some quick-stepping bird;
Not the blue or the gold of her own small cages,
Swept bare of all song now, sweet beyond words.

The concierge, breaking her bread in silence,
Sees sons returning from some great war.
The laughter crackles long after footsteps
Have dwindled down dank corridors.

Le Presbytère, Géay

The *curé*'s face is leering through
The window at the church he loved –
A dreary, greyish, ancient pile
Beloved of none but him above.

The breaths he takes are rasping, short.
His body's curiously bent awry.
Was he a taller man than this
When first he heard that voice – and sighed?

And did he rise up in his frame,
And square his jaw, and fix his eye
Upon a landscape strangely known
Already – though not outwardly?

And was it here that he began?
And is it here that he remained?
Must it be here that he will die
Before the winter rimes the pane?

La Tour Eiffel Parle . . .

I stand here with all four legs braced
Against the clamours of the hour,
Once *provisoire*, now *permanente*,
The greatest on the Champ de Mars.

All Paris is my *quartier* –
Mais oui, je suis le grand guetteur! –
I watch them in their restaurants,
Savouring eyes, lips, fingers, hair . . .

O, would that woman could be mine!
Says one, and, seeing him watching her,
She half-smiles an acknowledgement
Before her partner shifts his chair.

Mate checked, they concentrate on food,
Our gastronomic connoisseurs.
If man is shaped by what he eats,
They'll turn to something round and rare

When they have feasted of the best
La France has toiled to offer them –
Its cheeses, meats, its *bouillabaisse*
(If Paris may anoint the Sud . . .)

O how I love to love all this –
Cette ville – ma ville! – si chère, si chic . . .
I rise, as Doisneau caught me then,
And shimmy-shimmy from the hips . . .

III

Envoi

An Invitation

Do come and see my special sea.
I've coloured it all grey.
There is no other colour now.
The others wore away.

There was a boat that sailed on it.
I pulled the plug. It drowned
With two red, waving men on board
Who loved to sing and lounge.

No, they weren't sailors, those two men.
They didn't mean to go.
It wasn't their boat that they sailed.
It came up from below.

They saw it on the beach today,
Just drifting with the tide.
They loved the gorgeous look of it,
That yellow hull so smooth and wide . . .

'Paris 1945' p. 118

This poem is in part a loose, free-hand rendering of a paragraph from 'Mille Planches de Salut' (*Recherche de la base et du sommet*, René Char, p. 91, Gallimard, 1955)

'Fashioning Beginnings' p. 113

cf. Char, p. 75–6. Ditto as above

'Objet Trouvé Chez René' p. 115

See Char, p. 95, for the phrase 'l'éperon du jour et la paroi de la nuit'

'Vapours' p. 116

cf. Char, p. 77. Ditto as above

'Récit' p. 121

cf. Char, pp. 77–8. Ditto as above

'Perhaps One Would Have Spoken Thus In The Presence of Braque . . .' p. 124

cf. Char, p. 68. Ditto as above

'Poet & Painter' p. 128

cf. Char, 'Sous la Verrière', p. 58. Gist of explanation as above.